I SURVIVED

THE NAZI INVASION, 1944

I SURVIVED

THE SINKING OF THE *TITANIC*, 1912

THE SHARK ATTACKS OF 1916

HURRICANE KATRINA, 2005

THE BOMBING OF PEARL HARBOR, 1941

THE SAN FRANCISCO EARTHQUAKE, 1906

THE ATTACKS OF SEPTEMBER 11, 2001

THE BATTLE OF GETTYSBURG, 1863

THE JAPANESE TSUNAMI, 2011

THE NAZI INVASION, 1944

I SURVIVED

THE NAZI INVASION, 1944

by Lauren Tarshis

illustrated by Scott Dawson

Scholastic Inc.

ISBN 978-0-545-45938-9

20 19 18 17 16 17 18 19/0

Printed in the U.S.A. 40
First printing, January 2014
Designed by Tim Hall

This book is dedicated to the Jewish partisans of World War II, with special mention to those whose incredible life stories I discovered in my research and inspired the characters in this book:
Leizer and Zenia Bart, Miriam Brysk, Leon Kahn, Ben Kamm, Vitka Kempner, Ruzka Korczak, Abba Kovner, Miles Lerman, and Shalom Yoran

CHAPTER 1

AUGUST 10, 1944
LODA FOREST
EASTERN POLAND

All across Europe, Jewish people were being hunted.

Millions were already dead.

But eleven-year-old Max Rosen was determined to stay alive.

Max thought that he and his little sister, Zena, would be safe in this forest.

But now they were caught in a massive bombing attack.

German planes roared through the sky, dropping 1,000-pound bombs that fell with shattering explosions.

Kaboom!

Enormous trees became flaming torches.

Sparks showered down like burning snowflakes.

Twisted metal and razor-sharp shards of wood blew up all around them.

And this was only the beginning.

Soon, soldiers with machine guns would stampede through the forest, hunting for people who had survived the explosions and fires. Anyone they caught would be shot on the spot.

Max gripped Zena's hand and they ran for their lives. Their only hope was a nearby swamp. They could hide in the mud and slime, with the snakes and the snapping turtles and the razor-sharp grass.

But then came the biggest explosion of all.

KABOOM!

The force ripped Max away from Zena, and sent him flying through the air.

His body twisted and turned. His mind swirled with terror.

Smack!

He landed in a ditch. He lay there, dazed.

Was he still alive?

But then there was a thundering crack above.

Max looked up just in time to see a massive flaming tree crashing down on top of him.

CHAPTER 2

THREE DAYS EARLIER
THE JEWISH GHETTO
ESTIES, POLAND

Max and his nine-year-old sister, Zena, walked along the dark and dirty street, ignoring the rat that skittered by. They hadn't eaten since last night's watery potato soup, and they were hoping to find something for supper. They had no money and nothing left to trade. But they weren't ready to give up.

Suddenly two German soldiers appeared from around the corner, their boots clicking sharply on the stone sidewalk. Max and Zena jumped into the gutter. Max wanted to curse these men, spit at them, chase them out of his town. But he stood quietly, eyes down, clenching his fists as he waited for the soldiers to pass.

The men were Nazis, killer soldiers of Adolf Hitler, Germany's leader. Hitler had started a terrible war. He had sent his brutal armies to invade countries all over Europe. A year ago, Nazi soldiers marched into Esties, the Polish town where Max's family had lived for hundreds of years.

The Nazis came with their tanks, their machine guns — and their hatred of Jewish people like Max and Zena.

Hitler told hideous lies, blaming Jews for every problem in the world. In Esties, Nazi soldiers destroyed Jewish-owned businesses, including Papa's electrical repair shop. They set fire to the synagogue and ripped apart sacred Torah scrolls. They attacked Jewish people on the streets, including Dr. Latham, who had taken such good care of Mama before she died. What had Dr. Latham done to deserve a beating? He had dared to *look* at the soldiers as he walked by them.

Two months after the invasion, the Nazis forced all Jewish people to leave their homes. They all had to move to a ghetto — this bleak neighborhood of crumbling buildings on the edge of town. The ghetto was surrounded by a barbed wire fence, and patrolled by Nazi guards and policemen. It was like living in a jail.

But the worst was to come.

A month ago, in the middle of the night, policemen arrested Papa and dragged him away. They took dozens of other Jewish men, too. Nobody had any idea where they had been taken. But there were terrifying whispers — about gunshots echoing through the hills around the town, about locked trains that took Jewish people to prison camps.

Some said that this was happening all around Europe. There were rumors that hundreds of thousands of Jews had been taken away — and had never been heard from again.

Max didn't know what to believe.

All he knew was that each day, life seemed to get worse. He and Zena lived all alone now, in a small, dark room that stank of garbage. As life got harder and harder, Max thought of what his Aunt Hannah had said to him, just after the invasion. She'd put her hands on Max's shoulders, and looked at him with her glittering green eyes.

"The Nazis want to take everything from us," she'd said in her clear and certain voice. "Do not let them take away your hope."

Max looked around him now, at the woman limping past with tears in her eyes, at the ragged children slumped in the doorways.

Finding hope in the ghetto was harder than finding food.

Just then, Zena grabbed his arm.

“Max, look!” she said, pointing at a little bird perched on the barbed wire fence at the end of an alley.

“It’s a robin,” Zena said. “Don’t you know that robins are lucky birds?”

Max arched an eyebrow at his sister.

After all that had happened to them, did she really believe there was such a thing as a lucky bird?

But then he glimpsed something else, just behind the bird: a raspberry bush, covered with bright red berries.

Max stared, imagining the sweet fruit bursting in his mouth.

Zena saw them, too.

He and Zena rushed to the fence and dropped to their knees. They carefully stuck their arms between the wires, avoiding the razor-sharp barbs. They stretched their fingers, but couldn’t reach a single berry. The bush was just a few inches too far away.

Max looked around.

He could see no guards watching this area. And there was just enough space under the fence for Max to squeeze through. It was dangerous; anyone caught trying to leave the ghetto was arrested, or worse. But Max wasn't trying to escape. He would be outside the fence for just a minute or so.

"I'll be quick," he said to Zena.

"No," she said. Her blue eyes seemed to grab hold of him. With her blonde curls and round cheeks, people always said Zena looked like a doll. Sure — a doll made of steel. She was almost two years younger than Max, but he trusted her more than anyone else in the world.

"I'll get some for us to eat now," he said. "But I'll get extra so we can trade for more potatoes."

Zena thought for a moment, licking her lips as she eyed the berries.

She gave Max a grudging nod.

Before she could change her mind, Max was on his stomach, slithering under the fence. He picked a handful of berries, tossing one to Zena. She caught it and popped it into her mouth, breaking out into the biggest smile he'd seen in weeks.

But then her face crumbled.

The robin flew away.

Max turned just in time to see a Nazi soldier looming over him. Without a word, the man swung his rifle and smacked Max in the side of the head.

CHAPTER 3

The soldier marched Max along the dusty road leading away from the ghetto. He jabbed him in the spine with the sharp tip of his rifle, barking out German commands Max couldn't understand. They were heading toward town — to the police station, Max was sure. Nobody who was taken there had ever come back.

A Nazi flag flew above the building now, angry red with a black swastika — the twisted Nazi cross. Max could see it in the distance, a bloodstain on the blue sky.

Max's head throbbed from where the soldier had smacked him. But the pain was nothing compared to the fear that churned inside him. What would the Nazis do to him? And what would happen to Zena, alone in the ghetto?

The thought made him so weak he could barely walk. The soldier gave him a hard shove to keep him moving.

The road snaked along the river, and from the banks below Max heard laughter and splashing. The sound felt like a cold slap — he could not think of the last time he'd heard such happy noises. But he could remember so clearly those days before the war, when it had been Max and Zena splashing in the cool, clear river, with not one worry in their minds.

When they were younger, they'd play hide-and-seek with Papa. But sometimes they'd venture too far, and get themselves lost. They'd wander around, scared the forest would swallow them forever.

But then they'd hear Papa's voice, calling to them.

"Max, Zena, where are you?"

And Max and Zena would cry out, "Papa! We're here!"

And soon enough, Papa would appear, a smile on his face. And he always said the same thing.

"I knew I'd find you!"

The best times were when Aunt Hannah came along. She was Papa's sister, just nineteen years old. She'd always been more like a friend to Max than a fussy old aunt. She'd take Max and Zena on hikes, jumping with them from rock to rock, singing their favorite songs.

People in town gossiped about Hannah — that she was wild, that she cared more about books than finding a husband. Of course Max knew that Hannah didn't want to get married, not now. She was saving her money to go to America.

"We'll all go to America together," Aunt Hannah would say. "It will be an adventure!"

And Max would picture himself with Zena and Papa and Hannah, standing at the railing of a grand ship, looking out over the bright blue ocean.

But like everything else in Max's world, the Nazis had shattered that dream.

And where was Aunt Hannah now?

Max had no idea if she was even alive.

The last time he knew she was safe was just one day before they had to move into the ghetto.

It was late at night, and Hannah had come to their house. Max was almost asleep when he heard her voice. He'd almost leaped out of bed to see her.

But she and Papa were fighting, so Max stayed put.

"I'm going tonight," Hannah was saying. "We all must go!"

"Keep your voice down," Papa scolded.

Where was Aunt Hannah going?

Max strained his ears, but heard no more.

Finally he crept downstairs, hoping to talk to Aunt Hannah himself.

But she was gone.

And when Max went to her house the next day, there was no trace of her.

"Where did she go?" Max asked Papa.

Papa just shook his head, and he looked so sad Max decided not to ask again. And then Max figured it out: Aunt Hannah had managed to catch her ship to America. She had left them behind, without even saying good-bye.

Thinking of Aunt Hannah made Max's head throb even more as he trudged along the dusty road. He barely heard the rustling sound coming from the bushes.

But the soldier whirled around, his piglike eyes squinting into the thicket on the side of the road.

Max's blood froze when he saw a curly blonde head poking up through the bushes.

Zena!

She was crazy to come after him!

But of course he would have done the exact same crazy thing for her.

"Achtung!" the soldier barked.

He aimed his rifle at Zena, pulled back the bolt, and got ready to fire.

CHAPTER 4

"No!" Max screamed.

A strange new feeling boiled inside him, furious and black and powerful. It didn't matter that the soldier was big as an ox, that he had a rifle. Max's body seemed to move on its own, fueled by a mix of terror and fury.

With all of his might, Max threw himself against the man.

The soldier teetered for a second, and then fell with a furious grunt. The rifle flew out of his hands, sailing through the air. When it landed, the rifle butt hit a rock.

Crack!

The rifle fired!

The soldier shouted out in pain and grabbed his leg.

He'd been hit by his own bullet!

Max stood there, stunned, as he stared at the blood oozing through the soldier's fingers.

The man's eyes bulged with rage as he spat out German curses. He crawled toward his rifle, clawing the dirt with his fingers, dragging his bloody leg behind him.

Zena shrieked. "Max, come on!"

Her voice snapped Max out of his trance.

He ran to her. They joined hands and took off through the brush, away from the soldier and the ghetto. He had no idea where they could go. But neither of them looked back, and they moved so quickly it seemed as if they were flying. They pushed aside branches, dodged trees, and jumped over roots and rocks. Thorns raked their legs and

snagged their clothes. But they ran and ran until finally their bodies gave out.

"I need to rest," Zena gasped, reaching for Max's arm.

"Up there," Max wheezed. "We'll hide in that wheat field."

They staggered into the field, wading through the golden stalks until at last they collapsed to the ground.

They lay there, gulping at the air, trying to catch their breaths. It was a long time before Max's body stopped shaking, before either of them could speak.

Finally Zena turned to him.

"We beat them," she whispered.

Max looked at his sister, not sure what she meant.

But then he understood: Here they were, still alive, not shivering in a jail cell or surrounded by barbed wire.

Zena was right. They'd fought their own battle against the Nazis.

And they'd won.

Max smiled a little, feeling a small burst of power.

But it soon faded.

Because he had no idea what they would do next.

Where could they go?

The Nazis had invaded every country around Poland, and that blood-red swastika flag now flew over more than ten countries in Europe. For a Jew, there was no safe place for thousands of miles in any direction.

And it wasn't only the Nazis from Germany who wanted to hurt them.

Some people in Esties had joined the Nazis in their terror. This had shocked Max, even though he'd always known there were those in their town who looked down on Jewish people. Max remembered one night when he and Zena and Papa were heading to synagogue. They had passed two young men who cursed and spat at them as they walked by.

"Hey!" Max had shouted to them.

But Papa grabbed his arm, hurrying him along.

"Why did they do that?" Max asked.

"There is no reason," Papa answered.

"Why do they hate us?" Zena asked.

"Because they have small minds" was Papa's impatient reply. "It's as simple as that."

But Max had pushed back. "I don't understand, Papa. What did we do to them?"

"We did nothing," Papa said. "It's always been this way. Jews are different. And some people are suspicious of what they don't understand."

It made no sense. Why be cruel to someone just because they were different?

And were Jews *really* so different from everyone else?

Max thought of his best friends at school. Those boys were just like him! They loved baseball. *Tarzan* was their favorite comic. They stared at pretty girls but were afraid to talk to them. True, his friends went to church on Sundays and Max went to synagogue on Fridays and Saturdays. But it seemed like they were all learning the same things: to obey God, to respect their parents, to be honest and kind.

And yet Max had seen with his own eyes how some of his neighbors had smiled and cheered when the Jews were marched to the ghetto. Many of Esties's own policemen had helped burn down the synagogue, and were even more vicious than the Nazis.

It seemed to Max that Hitler had struck a match. With that little spark, old suspicions turned to blazing hatred.

Zena moved closer to Max now, putting her head on his shoulder.

"I need to close my eyes," she said groggily. "Just for a minute."

Seconds later, she was fast asleep.

Max gently wrapped his arm around his sister's bony shoulders, holding her tight.

It was dark now, and Max struggled to stay alert, to keep watch. But soon the sound of the rustling wheat lulled Max to sleep, too. His dreams carried him far away, until he found himself on a ship, in the middle of the ocean.

He stood with Zena, looking out over the water, a salty breeze cooling his face. He could hear Papa's warm laugh, and Aunt Hannah singing a happy song. Until a man's voice jarred him awake.

Max looked up, and his heart stopped.

There was a tough-looking old man standing over them, with a rifle.

"Get up now," the man said.

CHAPTER 5

The man wasn't dressed like a soldier; he was wearing work clothes, and his sunbaked face and roughened hands told Max he was a farmer, the man who must own this land.

Max and Zena stood up, and Max put himself between the farmer and Zena, ready for a fight.

But then Max noticed something about the man's craggy face, which was lit up by the moon.

His expression was tough. But his eyes looked at them with kindness.

"We must move now," he said in an urgent whisper. "The Nazis are already searching the farm. And more are coming."

And it hit Max.

This man wanted to help them!

Seconds later, the roar of truck engines shattered the quiet. Doors slammed and footsteps shook the ground.

The old farmer pointed to the barn behind the wheat field.

"They've already searched my barn," he said. "Move quickly. Keep your heads down."

"All these soldiers are searching for us?" Max asked.

There seemed to be hundreds of men!

"No," the farmer said. "They are searching for people who blew up a Nazi train tonight."

A Nazi train, blown up!

Could that be true?

And the people who had done it had gotten away?

The thought gave Max a jolt of excitement.

He and Zena hurried behind the farmer, running through the field with quiet steps.

When they got to the barn, the farmer slid the door open just enough for Max and Zena to slip inside.

"Go quickly up into the hayloft," he said, pointing to a ladder. "Move as far back as you can, near the wall. Cover yourselves with hay. Do not move, no matter what!"

Max met the old man's gentle eyes. No, not everyone had been infected by the Nazis' hate. He also realized how brave this man was, what a risk he was taking to help Max and Zena — two strangers. People caught hiding Jews were shot.

Max opened his mouth to thank him, but in a blink the barn door closed tight, and he and Zena were alone in the dark.

They scrambled blindly up the ladder leading to the hayloft. They had barely covered themselves with hay when they heard thundering voices just outside.

"Into the barn!" a man's voice boomed.

The barn door slammed open. Max peered through the hay. He glimpsed four men: the farmer and three Nazi soldiers.

And there was something else: a dog — a massive German shepherd. It growled and strained on a steel chain leash, its snarling teeth glowing in the light of the soldiers' flashlights.

Max dropped his head and inched closer to Zena, gluing himself to her side.

"Why are we here?" demanded the old farmer. "I helped the commander search this barn thirty minutes ago. The criminals are hiding in the wheat field."

His tone was gruff and bullying, almost as though he was in charge.

Max understood it was an act. But would he fool the other men?

"The dog led us to this barn," said a Nazi with a high, rasping voice.

"The barn is filled with cats," the farmer spat back. "Of course the dog wants to search!"

The dog's growls rose up.

Grrrrrrr.

Grrrrrr.

Terror chewed Max's insides.

"We're giving those criminals time to escape," the farmer insisted. "The commander will not be pleased! I will tell him how you wasted our time!"

Men murmured.

The dog's growling grew louder.

Grrrrr!

Grrrrr!

And finally the rasping man shouted out a command in German.

"Stille!"

The dog went silent.

"We will find those filthy Jews who destroyed our train," the man rasped. "And we will make them suffer for what they did."

Max shivered.

"We will never find them if we stay in this barn!" the farmer said. "Because of you, they will escape!"

Max held his breath.

"All right," the rasping man said. "To the fields!"

And in seconds, the men and the dog were gone.

Max and Zena lay there, frozen in fear, as minutes crawled into hours.

Voices echoed from the fields, engines roared. Max couldn't tell if people were coming or going, if they were getting closer or farther away. And just as he felt sure that he would be crushed by his own fear, the barn door slid open again. There was light, and footsteps, and the farmer's relieved face looking up at him.

He gave them a small, gruff smile.

"They're gone."

Max and Zena sat up, brushing pieces of hay from their hair.

The farmer climbed into the loft.

"Wait here," he said, walking to the back wall.

He took a knife from his back pocket and wedged it between two planks of wood.

What was happening?

A plank clattered to the floor, and the farmer stepped aside.

As Max and Zena stared in shock, three people stepped out of the small, dark opening.

Max made out the shadowy shapes of three men, each with a rifle slung over his shoulder.

One by one, they embraced the farmer.

"Jablonski," one said. "You are our angel."

"You are heroes," the farmer — Jablonski — said. "That train was carrying even more weapons than we had thought. It's all destroyed. The mission was a complete success."

It took a moment for Max to understand: These were the men who had blown up the train!

"Who are they?" said another man, noticing Max and Zena.

"I haven't exactly figured that out yet," Mr. Jablonski said, putting a gentle hand on Zena's head. "But I'd say they're good guys."

The men stepped forward to meet them. But before Max could think, or even take a breath, the smallest of the three men gasped. He dropped his rifle and threw his arms around Max and Zena.

And that's when Max realized this person wasn't a man.

It was Aunt Hannah.

CHAPTER 6

The men left the barn quietly, leaving Aunt Hannah, Max, and Zena alone with their hugs and tears. Max and Zena told her about their escape from the brutal Nazi soldier and how Mr. Jablonski had rescued them.

Aunt Hannah listened with wide eyes, gripping their hands.

"Where is your papa?" she asked.

Max and Zena both looked down.

"The Nazis took him," Max said finally. "A month ago."

"We don't know where he is," Zena told her.

Aunt Hannah seemed to stop breathing. It was a long moment before she spoke.

"I wanted us all to escape together," she said softly. "I begged your papa. But he refused. He said it was too dangerous. Like most people, he wanted to believe that if we just went along with the Nazis, things would be okay. He didn't want to accept the truth — that the Nazis are more evil than we could have ever imagined."

Aunt Hannah's words seemed to burrow deep into Max's mind, to a place where he kept his darkest fears. And in a flash, he understood: that all of those rumors he'd heard in the ghetto were true. The Nazis were cold-blooded killers.

"Your papa and I had the most terrible fights," she said.

Max remembered the argument he'd overheard, and Aunt Hannah's pleading words.

"We all must go."

"And then it was too late," Aunt Hannah said.

"I never even got to say good-bye, to tell you where I was going."

"Where *did* you go?" Max asked.

"There are Jews hiding in the forests who are fighting back against the Nazis," she said. "There are hundreds of them. I joined them."

"You're a soldier?" Zena asked, her eyes wide.

"Not a regular soldier," Aunt Hannah said.

She explained that she was a partisan, a special kind of fighter. She did not belong to a real army, with uniforms and shining weapons. They could not go into battle against the Nazis — they didn't stand a chance against the German Panzer tanks and bombers and heavy machine guns.

Instead, they worked in small groups, plotting surprise attacks.

They blew up trains loaded with supplies and weapons, burned down factories that made German uniforms and guns, and ambushed troops in daring nighttime raids.

Aunt Hannah said there were hundreds of

partisan groups hiding in the forests around Poland and other countries in the east. Not all partisans were Jewish, but everyone in Aunt Hannah's group was, including Martin and Lev, the two men here with her.

Altogether there were twenty-four fighters in Aunt Hannah's group, she explained. Most were young men. But there were some older people too, and four other women besides Aunt Hannah. They lived together in a hideout deep in Loda Forest, an endless stretch of pitch-black woods about fifteen miles north of here.

Max stared at his aunt as she talked.

She had the same glittering green eyes he remembered so well.

But Aunt Hannah had changed, and it wasn't just her chopped hair and her man's shirt and trousers. Her dreamy expression had hardened into one of toughness and determination.

Aunt Hannah was no longer a carefree teenager from Esties.

She was fighting the Nazis!

But was it really possible for a group of ragtag soldiers to take on the entire Germany military? Hitler had millions of soldiers fighting for him!

Then Max thought of a Bible story he'd loved when he was little — about the Jewish boy David who'd fought against the monstrous warrior Goliath.

The Jews were in the middle of a war back then, too, fighting against their most feared enemy, the Philistines. And Goliath was the most terrifying Philistine warrior of all. He stood nine feet tall, with the finest bronze armor and sharpest sword and javelin.

Goliath taunted the Jews, daring them to send their toughest soldiers to fight him. But nobody would accept Goliath's challenge. Even the most famous Jewish warriors said it was hopeless, that no Jew stood a chance against Goliath.

But David refused to believe that. He wasn't a soldier, just a shepherd. He didn't have armor or a sword, only a slingshot. But he was fierce and smart and determined to fight.

Goliath just laughed when skinny David stepped up to fight him.

But then David shot at him with his slingshot. One small rock struck Goliath in the head. Goliath fell to the ground. David lunged forward and grabbed Goliath's sword and — *whack!* — he chopped off Goliath's head. The Jews soon won the war, and David became their king.

Looking at Aunt Hannah now, as she gripped her battered rifle, Max thought she looked every bit as fierce as David must have. And a feeling came over him, as if he'd found something he'd lost, something precious.

His hope.

Max had a million more questions to ask Aunt Hannah, but there was no time.

"It's a long trip back to the forest," she said. "We have to leave soon."

Max understood that "we" meant him and Zena, too.

As Aunt Hannah led the way to Mr. Jablonski's farmhouse, Zena leaned over to whisper in Max's ear.

"That robin *did* bring us luck," she said.

Max had almost forgotten all about that little bird, perched on the ghetto barbed wire. He'd never been the type to believe in lucky birds.

Maybe now he was.

CHAPTER 7

They all sat together around Mr. Jablonski's scratched wooden table. It was covered with more food than Max or Zena had seen in a year. There was nothing fancy, just bread, cheese, apples, and a pitcher of frothy milk. But to Max it looked like a holiday feast. Mr. Jablonski filled two plates for Max and Zena, and neither of them even tried to remember their manners. They gobbled their food, washing down huge mouthfuls with gulps of milk.

Mr. Jablonski kept refilling their plates as

Martin and Lev looked on with smiles. The men acted as if Max and Zena were part of their families, too.

Martin was the youngest of the group — he looked about seventeen. He was as big as a bear, with a quick laugh. Lev seemed to be just a little older than Aunt Hannah, small but very muscular. His round glasses gave him a shy and bookish look. But his eyes were steely, and Max could see by the way the others listened to him that he was the leader of their little group.

Mr. Jablonski wasn't Jewish or a partisan — he was a spy. He'd tricked the Nazis into thinking he loved Hitler. He'd even become close friends with the Nazi commander in the area. But secretly he was working with the partisans — helping plot their missions, hiding them in his barn, supplying them with food and news from the outside.

After Max and Zena finished eating, Lev spread a map across the table. He traced their route back to the forest. If they were lucky, they'd reach their camp by sundown tomorrow night.

They also talked about the war, showing Max and Zena on the map where the latest battles were being fought. In the ghetto, newspapers and radios had been forbidden. Nobody had any real idea about what was happening outside the barbed wire fence. The Nazis always made it seem as though they were crushing their enemies, and that any day Hitler would be the leader of the entire world.

But now Max and Zena learned the amazing truth — Germany was losing the war!

The Nazis still controlled most of the countries in Europe, but their grip was slipping. American and British forces were battering them in France and other areas to the west. But the real trouble for the Nazis was on the other side of the map, in Russia.

Lev pointed to that giant country, which stretched out to Poland's east.

"Hitler has sent millions of German soldiers to Russia," Lev said. "He figured the Russians would surrender within a few weeks."

But the Russians were determined fighters, and the battles dragged on and on. By now, German troops were running low on weapons, food, and warm clothes.

The Nazis kept loading up trains with supplies. But few of these trains made it to Russia.

"We're blowing them all up," Martin said, flashing a smile.

Different partisan groups were targeting trains all over the east. Lately they'd been destroying hundreds of trains every *week*.

"But tonight's train was one of the most important," Lev told them.

It had more than thirty railcars, packed with machine guns, tons of ammunition, and winter uniforms. But most important: Panzer tanks.

"There were twenty of them," Martin added.

Max shuddered as he remembered the enormous steel beasts rumbling through the streets of Esties, their guns powerful enough to blast away an entire building in one shot. For weeks after the invasion, Max had nightmares that a Panzer was chasing him. He'd wake up drenched in sweat, his arms and legs aching as though he'd been running for his life.

To destroy the train, Aunt Hannah, Lev, and Martin had carried a fifty-pound explosive from their base in the forest. They traveled in the dead of night, dodging Nazi soldiers guarding the tracks. They climbed onto a train bridge that stretched across two high ridges, and tied the bomb to the underside of the tracks.

Then they hid behind a rock, readied the bomb's detonator, and waited for the train.

Hours passed.

But then, finally . . .

Whoooooooooooooooo!

Whoooooooooooooooo!

The train barreled toward the bridge. Black smoke belched from the stack of the massive locomotive. A Nazi flag glowed in the moonlight. And there were the Panzer tanks, each sitting on its own flatbed railcar. Behind them, an endless line of railcars was packed with supplies for the Nazi troops.

The train approached the bridge.

With a flick of a finger, Lev triggered the blast.

Kaboom!

The bomb exploded in a massive ball of fire.

In a flash, the bridge crumbled, its wooden supports snapping like toothpicks.

The train's locomotive seemed to hang helplessly in the air for a moment. And then it started its plunge into the rocky valley hundreds of feet below.

One by one, the train's dozens of cars followed the engine in its deadly fall.

Crash!

Boom!

Crash!

And then,

Kaboom!

Tons of ammunition exploded in a tower of fire that shot up thousands of feet into the air.

Max could picture it all in his mind — the train's dive from the bridge, the smoldering wreckage, the Nazi flag bursting into flames.

Thinking about it gave him a jolt of excitement — and also fear.

He thought of that Nazi soldier with the rasping voice, standing in the barn with his ferocious dog. He remembered his chilling threat.

"We will make them suffer for what they did."

Max looked out the window into the black night.

It would be a long and dangerous journey back to the forest.

And suddenly he wondered what would be waiting for them there.

CHAPTER 8

LATER THAT NIGHT
EN ROUTE TO LODA FOREST,
EASTERN POLAND.

Lev led the way, taking them on a zigzagging route along the river, through fields of wheat and rye, and pastures filled with cows and sheep. Aunt Hannah walked between Max and Zena, her eyes narrowed and rifle aimed, her finger glued to the trigger.

They stayed hidden, avoiding towns, ducking into bushes at the slightest sound — a dog barking, a baby crying, a wagon clattering down a distant road.

It was just past sunrise when they finally reached the edge of Loda Forest.

They pushed their way through a wall of thick, thorny bushes, and suddenly they were in a completely new world.

Enormous trees towered all around them, their branches forming a roof that blocked out all but a few beams of sunlight. Moss hung from branches, and giant, twisted roots rose up from the muddy ground. Max had heard horror stories about Loda when he was a child — about packs of wolves and bloodthirsty bandits. He looked nervously into the shadows, half expecting a hairy arm to reach out and snatch him.

But Aunt Hannah, Martin, and Lev walked with sure steps, as though this tangled wilderness was their backyard. Soon Max's eyes adjusted to the darkness, and he got used to the forest sounds — the buzzing and chirping and hooting, the rushing of the streams, the snapping of twigs under their feet.

He thought of Papa, and those games of hide-and-seek, when Max and Zena were sure they were lost forever. And then they'd hear Papa's voice calling to them.

He could almost hear it now, from somewhere far away.

"Max, Zena, where are you?"

Max slowed his steps, turning his head, as though the whispering breeze were Papa's voice.

He wanted to climb high into a tree and scream out, at the top of his lungs.

"We're here, Papa!"

The words seemed to ring out from his thoughts — *We're here.*

He looked around, as though any second Papa's smiling face might appear through the leaves.

"I knew I'd find you!"

As they got deeper into the forest, the group walked more slowly, making doubly sure that nobody was following them. Lately the Nazis were desperate to capture partisans, Aunt Hannah explained, to track them to their secret camps. They sent search planes buzzing over the forest, like giant birds hunting for prey. Many camps had been discovered and destroyed, their members all killed.

"But they'll never find us," Martin said defiantly.

Their camp was tucked away on an island that rose up in the middle of a great swamp, Lev told them. Their sleeping huts were dug into the ground, the rooftops covered with dirt and grass. They'd built a bridge of fallen trees that led across the swamp to the island. But they'd sunk the bridge down under a few inches of water so that nobody could see it.

"It sounds like a movie," Max said, turning to smile at Zena.

But Zena stared at the ground, and suddenly Max realized something was very wrong with her.

Her face was twisted in pain, her eyes brimming with tears.

"What is it?" Max said, barely hiding his panic. Aunt Hannah stopped, too.

Was Zena sick?

Diseases were everywhere in the ghetto — coughs that turned people to skeletons, burning fevers that wiped out whole families in days.

"It's my toe," Zena admitted finally.

It had to be bad to make Zena cry.

They found a fallen tree and sat Zena down. Everyone huddled around as Aunt Hannah knelt down and gently removed Zena's boot.

Zena gritted her teeth as Aunt Hannah peeled away her blood-soaked sock. Max's stomach lurched at the sight of her big toe — the skin was torn away, the nail almost completely ripped off.

Aunt Hannah didn't flinch.

"It's just that your boot is too small," she said. "It's not bad at all."

Lev nodded in agreement. "I've seen way worse."

Aunt Hannah stood up. "Look at this," she said, lifting her pant leg. "Barbed wire," she said, pointing at a purple, jagged scar. "We set fire to a bullet factory, and I got caught on our way out."

Max cringed.

"Mine's uglier," Martin said, pushing up his sleeve. His forearm looked as if it had been torn open and sewn back together by a three-year-old.

"Grenade," he said proudly. "Went off a little too soon."

"Show them your scar, Lev," Aunt Hannah said daringly.

Martin leaned forward and whispered loudly to Zena.

"Lev got shot in the rear end," he said with a laugh.

"Hey," Lev said with a frown that looked only half serious. "That's supposed to be my secret."

They all laughed, including Lev — and Zena.

Aunt Hannah opened her canteen and poured some water over Zena's toe. Lev took his knife and cut open the toe of Zena's boot, turning it into a sandal.

Zena slipped it on, and stood up.

"Better," she said with relief.

And on they marched.

The swamp was just coming into view when Martin suddenly stopped short.

"What?" Lev asked.

Martin looked around, his rifle raised.

"Do you hear that?" he asked.

And then Max heard it, too, a faint buzzing sound.

But it wasn't coming from inside the forest.

It was coming from above.

Max looked up, his heart hammering.

The buzzing got louder and louder, until it turned into a roar.

"Bombers!" Martin shouted.

There was a whining sound, and then a massive explosion behind them.

Kaboom!

"It's an attack!" Lev screamed. "The Nazis are bombing the forest!"

CHAPTER 9

Max dove into the dirt, pulling Zena down with him just as the forest seemed to erupt into flames.

Kaboom!

Kaboom!

Kaboom!

Branches flew through the air like fiery torches.

Sparks rained down on them, burning through their clothes and sizzling against their skin.

Max lay there, frozen with fear, holding Zena as tightly as he could.

"Max!" she gasped. "You're crushing me! I can't breathe!"

He loosened his grip, but not by much.

The smoke stung his eyes and burned his lungs.

The worst was the noise, the roaring of the planes, the whistling of the falling bombs, and then the thundering, bone-rattling explosions.

Max could just barely see the planes through the cover of the trees.

But from the sound he could tell they were Junkers, the Nazis' most feared bombers. Max had seen them in the weeks after the invasion, streaking over Esties, low enough that he could see their pilots' piercing eyes. Papa told him they were the fastest bombers in the Nazi fleet, with six machine guns. Each plane could carry thousands of pounds of bombs.

"We can't stay here!" Martin said. "We need to leave the forest!"

"No!" Lev said. "That's what they want us to do. I'm sure the Nazis have the forest surrounded now. They're trying to flush us out so they can capture us as we try to escape."

"You're right," Aunt Hannah said. "First they will drop bombs. And then they will send in troops."

So this was just the beginning.

"We need to get to the swamp," Lev said. "We can hide in the grass. And then to the camp."

"What if they bomb the island, too?" Martin asked.

The question hung in the air, and Lev had no answer.

But Aunt Hannah spoke up, her eyes flashing.

"The Nazis have no idea that island even exists," she insisted. "The camp will be safe. And we will get there."

As usual, there was not a hint of doubt in her words.

"Of course," Lev said. "Let's go!"

They started running toward the swamp, but Zena's cut-open boot made it hard for her to keep up. So Martin grabbed her arms and hoisted her up onto his back. She held on tight as he sprinted in the lead. Max followed at his heels, keeping his head low.

The bombs kept falling, shaking the ground, sending needles of wood flying through the sky. They sliced right through their clothes. One hit Max on the face, barely an inch from his eye.

But then Max could see the swamp. It was enormous, an endless sea of brown, soupy water. It was choked with grass and twisting trees. Max tried not to think of the slimy, poisonous creatures that lived there.

But anything was better than bombs.

Martin put Zena down, and she grabbed Max's hand. Martin started to wade into the swamp.

But seconds later, a plane swooped low over the trees.

Kaboom!

An invisible hand seemed to grab Max and hurl him into the air. Suddenly he was flying backward, his body twisting and turning.

Until *smack*, he landed in a ditch.

He sat there, stunned and dazed.

Was he alive?

He moved his arms and legs, blinked his eyes, and cleared his mind.

Amazingly, he was not hurt.

But then he heard a cracking sound.

He looked up just in time to see a flaming tree crashing down on top of him.

CHAPTER 10

Max quickly flipped onto his stomach. He flattened himself against the ground, bracing for the crushing blow.

The tree landed with a thunderous crash. The earth trembled. Dirt flew into Max's eyes and nose.

But the ditch was just deep enough so that Max was not smashed. The tree completely covered the ditch, but it had not hit him. It seemed that the fire was snuffed out when the tree fell.

Now he was just trapped.

He lay there, his drumming heart ready to burst from his chest.

Above him, Max heard footsteps and voices frantically calling his name.

He screamed for help, but his voice was a muffled whisper.

He realized nobody could see him.

And soon the voices faded, and he was alone.

He tried pushing against the tree with his back.

It didn't budge.

He remembered a few years ago, when there was a fierce thunderstorm in Esties. The lashing winds had knocked down dozens of trees. A branch from a giant oak had fallen in front of their house. It was only a branch, but Papa had needed the help of three other men to haul it away.

There was no way Max would be able to move the enormous tree.

It was hopeless.

Max lay in the ditch, facedown in the dirt.

It seemed as though the earth was swallowing him up, that he would soon disappear forever.

And for a split second, Max thought of just closing his eyes and letting the darkness take him.

But a voice — his own — shouted at him.

Get up!

Of course he couldn't just lie here and give in! He refused to let the Nazis beat him — at least not without a fight.

He clenched his teeth and managed to inch himself onto his side.

Somehow he had to find another way out of the ditch.

He groped around with his fingers, until he found a rock. He gripped it in his hand. It was small, but sharp — perfect for digging.

Max jammed the rock into the side of the ditch, scraping and digging, The work was agonizingly slow at first, and it was broiling hot. Sweat soaked his clothes and dripped into his eyes.

But soon he had carved out a small space. He

dug and dug, until he finally broke through to the surface. Fresh air poured in, cooling Max's face and giving him a second wind.

The dirt became looser, and Max dug more easily. He slipped the rock into his shirt pocket; he might need it later. Then he started grabbing the earth with his hands.

And finally he had made a hole that looked just big enough to squirm through.

He pushed with all of his might, worming himself under the tree. He ignored the splinters of wood that ripped into his skin.

He crawled out, feeling as though he had escaped from his own grave.

Max stood on wobbly legs, wiping the clumps of dirt from his ears and nose. His entire body ached; his fingertips were raw and bleeding.

He had no idea how long he'd been in the ditch — he guessed an hour at least.

He looked around, praying he'd see Zena and Aunt Hannah and Martin and Lev waiting for him.

But he was alone.

He looked out at the swamp. Had they gone there without him?

No, Max decided. They wouldn't leave him.

At least the bombs had stopped falling, and the skies were quiet.

But now Max heard a noise in the distance:

Rat, tat, tat.

Rat, tat, tat, tat.

There was no mistaking it: machine-gun fire.

The bombing was over.

The Nazi troops were now marching through the forest.

CHAPTER 11

Max swallowed hard, gathering up his courage.

It was all he could do to stop himself from diving back into his ditch. But if he had any hope of finding Zena and the others, he had to do it now. Already there must be soldiers in the forest. Soon they would be everywhere.

He had no idea where to begin. He figured they wouldn't have gone far from where they'd last been together. So he turned and started to walk.

He focused his senses, scanning all around him the way Aunt Hannah and Lev and Martin did, checking over his shoulder to make sure he wasn't being followed.

And then, up ahead, he made out the shapes of two men — Nazi soldiers.

He turned to flee, but something made him pause.

He ducked behind a tree and watched them. One of the men was walking with his pistol raised and aimed, as though he was a hunter stalking a deer.

Max followed the man's gaze. . . .

And there, crouched by a fallen tree, were Martin and Zena. They had their backs to the soldiers, with no idea they were in danger.

Max looked around frantically.

What could he do?

And then he remembered the rock.

He grabbed it from his pocket.

"Hey!" he screamed.

The soldiers turned and looked at Max.

The man who had been aiming the gun was enormous. He looked Max up and down and sneered at him, the way Goliath must have first looked at David.

That boiling rage Max had felt earlier came back to him, powering his muscles.

He gripped the rock, and with all of his might, he hurled it at the sneering soldier's head.

It flew through the air, a straight shot.

Thwack.

It hit the soldier squarely on the forehead.

The man stood in shock, then stumbled backward.

And now Martin was on his feet, his rifle aimed.

Crack!

He shot that soldier dead.

But there was the other soldier, and Martin aimed his rifle again.

He pulled the trigger.

Click.

The rifle was jammed!

Martin fumbled with it, tugging at the lever and cursing under his breath.

Meanwhile, the other soldier stood there, staring at Max.

He was small and skinny, and he looked very young, maybe just a few years older than Max. His uniform hung on him like it was three sizes too big. He reminded Max of some of his older friends from school, boys he had played cards with, traded comics with, raced on the playground.

Max and the young soldier stared at each other, their eyes locked together.

There was no hatred in the other boy's eyes. He looked just as terrified and confused as Max was.

Were they really enemies?

Or were they just two boys caught in this net of evil?

Martin had readied his rifle. He pulled back the bolt and took aim at the young soldier.

"No!" Max screamed.

Crack!

Max was too late — the bullet hit the young soldier in the chest. And as he fell dead to the ground, his arm jerked.

His pistol fired.

A split second later, the bullet tore into Max's side with a searing, blinding pain.

Max stared down in shock as blood gushed from the gaping wound.

He dropped to his knees.

Zena screamed out his name. Her voice echoed through his mind as the world spun all around him and then went dark.

Max lay in the dirt. Martin and Zena looked down at him.

They spoke to him, but he couldn't hear. His whole body felt numb. The gunfire and the shouts around him grew faint. Max closed his eyes, and soon he had drifted away from the burning forest, from the war, from the fear and the pain. He thought of that young soldier, and felt himself moving closer to him.

But from somewhere else, he heard Zena calling him. He felt her gripping his hand, as though she was trying with all of her might to pull him back to her.

But it wasn't until the next day when Max finally opened his eyes that he realized he had made it back — that unlike the scared young soldier, Max was still alive.

CHAPTER 12

FIVE WEEKS LATER

JEWISH PARTISAN CAMP

LODA FOREST

Max sat up in bed, his heart pounding with fear.

It was the same every morning — he kept thinking he was still in that ditch.

It always took him a moment to realize where he was, and that he and Zena were safe.

They were in their underground sleeping hut. Six men snored around them, their rifles by their sides. Zena snuffled softly on the tiny bed of logs she shared with Max. He reached and rested his hand lightly on her arm.

She sat up and rubbed her eyes, smiling at him.

"Today's the day," she whispered.

Aunt Hannah, Lev, and Martin were due back from a mission, their first since the attack in the forest. They had gone back toward Esties, to get some supplies from Mr. Jablonski.

Max followed Zena up a short ladder that led to the overhead door of the hut. He winced in pain as he hoisted himself out the door.

His wound was almost healed. The purple, puckered scar was even grislier than the ones Aunt Hannah and Martin had shown them. Dr. Zelman, the partisan doctor, kept telling Max how lucky he'd been. The bullet had lodged between two of his ribs. An inch in either direction and he wouldn't have survived.

Zena had told him the details of those hours after he'd been shot — how Martin had packed the wound with strips of fabric torn away from his own shirt, how he and Zena had stayed there, hiding in the bushes, praying that Max would survive.

Max remembered none of it.

But he'd heard the story of that day and night over and over, and he could picture it all in his mind.

After Martin had bandaged Max's wound, he'd hoisted him onto his back and led Zena to a large crater created by one of the bombs. He covered it with pine branches and they hid there as the soldiers swarmed around them. They stayed there for hours, until it was dark. Max was groaning in pain, and he seemed to be fading. Martin knew they needed to find a doctor as soon as possible, that he had to try to get them back to the camp.

And so once again, Martin put Max onto his back. He took Zena's hand. They crept through the burning darkness, dodging behind trees when they heard footsteps. There was no way to get to the underwater bridge — it was more than a mile away. They would have to cross the swamp in the water.

This was the part of the story that was hardest for Zena to tell; her blue eyes always grew shadowy with fear.

The water had been freezing cold, and the knifelike swamp grasses had sliced through their clothes. Snakes slithered between their legs, and sharp-toothed creatures nipped at them. But the worst was the mud, which at times came up past Zena's waist. Once, she became stuck, and it took all of Martin's strength to pull her out.

Finally it was too dangerous to keep going in the dark. They stopped in a cluster of dead trees that rose from the water like twisted skeletons. The forest glowed eerily around them, machine-gun fire pounded in the distance. And then came the most terrifying moment, when an enormous creature came floating through the water toward them.

But it turned out to be Hannah and Lev, gripping a giant branch.

The small group waited together until the sun came up, and then finally made it to the island. As Aunt Hannah had predicted, the camp had escaped the bombing. And within minutes, Max was in the hands of Dr. Zelman, an older partisan who had been a famous surgeon before he became a fighter. He removed the bullet, stitched the wound, and pumped Max full of medicines.

Through it all, Zena refused to leave her brother's side. Over the next few days, whenever Max woke up, he saw different people staring down at him — men with tangled beards, women with short-cropped hair, all looking at him with caring, worried eyes. And always the face closest to his was Zena's

Miraculously, Max was feeling better within a couple of weeks. Soon he and Zena were swept into the bustling life of the camp. His favorite times were sitting around the fire with the partisans, listening to them talk. Mostly they talked of the rumors about the war: that the Russians had finally chased the Nazis out of their country.

Now Russian soldiers were in eastern Poland, pushing the Nazis out. Hitler's troops were on the run.

The partisans spoke with cautious hope about the end of the war, about returning home. But Max saw the questions in their eyes: Exactly what was left of their homes . . . and their families?

They were all hoping that Aunt Hannah, Martin, and Lev would return with news.

And sure enough, later in the morning, the guard shouted down from his treetop lookout.

"They're back!" he called.

Max and Zena raced to the edge of the swamp and looked out over the sunken bridge.

There was Aunt Hannah, wading through the water, with Martin and Lev right behind her.

And there was someone else: a man.

At first, Max was sure he was dreaming.

He blinked, expecting that the man would disappear when he opened his eyes again.

But Zena saw him, too.

And soon they were both screaming.

"Papa!" they screamed. "Papa, we're here!"

They rushed into the water, not feeling the cold or the grass.

"We're here!"

And then they were in his arms. They held on with every ounce of strength they had.

It wouldn't be until later that Papa would tell them his story — how he'd escaped from a train that was taking him and thousands of other Jews to certain doom, how he'd made his way back to Esties.

The Nazis were gone — and so was everyone in the ghetto. There was not one soul left there.

Papa learned that they'd all been taken away. Just days after Max and Zena had escaped, everyone in the ghetto was put on a train.

Papa had searched everywhere for Max and Zena, refusing to believe they were lost.

And then, someone told him about an old farmer who'd rescued two children from his wheat field.

Mr. Jablonski.

There was so much to tell, but now was not the time.

None of them could speak through their tears of joy.

Until, finally, Papa leaned back, looking down at them. He opened his mouth, but it was a moment before he could say the words.

"I knew I would find you."

CHAPTER 13

TWO AND A HALF YEARS LATER

JANUARY 1947

ABOARD THE *ANNA MARINE*

THE ATLANTIC OCEAN

Max stood with Zena at the ship's railing, shivering in the cold. Papa sat on a chair behind them, his head bent over the book of English words they'd all been studying.

Suddenly, he looked up and called out to them. "See anything yet?"

“No, Papa,” said Zena.

“Keep looking,” Papa said with a smile. “Any minute now you’ll see land.”

This is what Papa had been saying all day. They’d been at sea for an entire week, and they were supposed to be arriving in New York soon. But as Max stared ahead, squinting into the bright sun, all he could see was the endless ocean.

Would they ever get to America?

It had been nearly two years since the end of the war, and even longer since they’d left Loda Forest.

Hitler was dead. Thousands of Nazis were locked up. Much of Europe was in ruins. Germany had been practically destroyed by bombers from America and England.

Everything was different now, and still changing.

Hannah and Lev were married and living in Palestine. Martin had gone with them. They were all helping build a new Jewish nation —

Israel. Thousands of Jewish people were already there. And Aunt Hannah had almost convinced Papa that he and Max and Zena should go to Palestine with them. But Papa knew how hard life would be for the settlers of that new nation. He'd decided America was the place for him and Max and Zena. Max would never forget the sadness of saying good-bye to Aunt Hannah and Lev and Martin.

"We will see each other soon!" Aunt Hannah had promised, in her bright and certain voice. But her glittering eyes were overflowing with tears as they hugged good-bye, and they all knew it could be a very long time before they were together again.

Papa, Max, and Zena stayed with Mr. Jablonski, but there was nothing left for them in Esties. Almost every Jewish person was gone forever, their lives stolen by the Nazis. There seemed to be ghosts everywhere, stains of the terrible things that had happened. Max was sad to say good-bye to Mr. Jablonski. But he was happy to leave Esties. He never wanted to go back.

They wandered for months, from city to city, crowded train after crowded train. They were part of a sea of Jewish survivors, hundreds of thousands of people with no homes, no money, and nowhere to go.

Finally they made their way to Rome, Italy. They stayed at small camp with hundreds of other Jews like them. The people working at the camp were volunteers who came from all over the world. A kind woman from America helped Papa write a letter to his cousin Saul, who lived in New York. The only way to get to America was if you had the help of a family member who already lived there. It had taken months for the letter to reach Saul, and several more for his response to get back to Papa.

"I will do anything and everything to help you, my dear cousin," he wrote.

Saul had a wife named Jennie, three grown

children, and six grandchildren who were around Max and Zena's age.

"We will all be waiting for your ship," Saul wrote in his last letter. "Your entire family is here for you. We will help you start your new life."

New life.

New life.

Max had said those words over and over to himself, not sure what they meant.

He wanted to forget all of the bad things that had happened, the fear and the sadness that he'd worn like a second skin, the evil of the Nazis, the suffering of those all around him, people who had lived through far worse than what he had experienced.

But could he really forget?

Was it right to forget?

Could Max really start a new and happy life after all that had happened?

For months before this voyage, he'd wrestled with these questions.

But then, just a few days before they boarded the ship, Max had been getting dressed. His eyes lingered on his scar. He'd almost forgotten about it. Sometimes the wound ached a little, but it had healed. Max ran his fingers across the puckered skin.

And it came to him — that the Nazis had wounded him in other places, too, places he couldn't see.

In his heart. In his mind.

He had scars there, too. And he would carry those scars with him for his whole life.

They would remind him of all of the terrible things that had happened, the sadness and the pain, the evil and the suffering he had witnessed.

But he would also remember the kindness of people like Mr. Jablonski, who risked his life to help them. He'd remember the incredible luck of finding Aunt Hannah — and then being reunited with Papa. He'd remember the bravery of the partisans, and how he and Zena never left each other's side. And he'd feel the strength inside him — and the hope — that had gotten him through these impossible years.

The ship seemed to be moving faster now, cutting through the waves. The sun was bright, the breeze salty and fresh, just like in Max's dreams.

When he got tired of standing he went to be with Papa, who scooted over to make room on his chaise. Papa put his arm around Max, and they studied the English book together.

Until Zena called to them.

"Max! Papa! I see it! I see America!"

Max and Papa jumped up. Max stood close to Zena, gripping her hand.

Papa stood behind them, one hand on each of their shoulders.

They looked out into the distance, and there it was: America.

All they could see at first was a thin black wisp on the horizon.

Zena turned to Max and smiled. Papa squeezed his shoulder.

They stood there together, looking ahead.

With every passing moment, what was up ahead seemed clearer and brighter.

It was waiting for them.

Their future.

A FEW MORE THOUGHTS AND FACTS

The events in this book, part of what is known as the Holocaust, are among the most terrible in all of history. I'm Jewish, and I remember first learning about Hitler and the Nazis when I was about your age. It's all so frightening to think about. There were times while I was writing this book when I wondered if the subject was just too horrifying to include in the I Survived series.

But many hundreds of you asked for a story on this topic. And so I decided to do my best to write about the Holocaust in a way that wasn't simply terrifying. I wanted to create a story that would inspire you. I wanted to help you begin to understand what happened. My hope is that you'll think about my story after you read it. I want you to talk about it with your parents, your teachers, and your friends.

Because by learning about the Holocaust — thinking about it, talking about it — you honor the memories of those who died and the millions of others who suffered. You also realize how lucky we are to live in a place where so many different kinds of people can live together peacefully. You already know it's wrong to be cruel to someone because they're different. The Holocaust shows what happens when people forget that, when hatred and prejudice explode out of control.

Like all of the stories in the I Survived series, this is a work of historical fiction. That means that all of the facts are true. I do tons of research to learn everything I can about a topic. And then I spin these facts into a story by adding characters and locations and a plot from my imagination.

But while my characters in this book are fictional, they are all based on real people, Jewish partisans I read about. These people amaze and inspire me. I hope you read more about them. You will be dazzled by their strength and spirit.

It was an enormous challenge to try to tell this story in ninety pages. As usual, I wish I could come visit all of you to talk more about what I learned, and to hear your questions and thoughts. Maybe someday! Instead, in the next pages I've done my best to answer the questions that are most likely on your mind. If you have more, please email me at LaurenTarshisAuthor@gmail.com.

Lauren Tarshis

QUESTIONS AND ANSWERS ABOUT WORLD WAR II, THE HOLOCAUST, AND THE PARTISAN FIGHTERS IN EUROPE

How many Jewish people became partisans?

There were about one million partisan fighters in World War II — men and women from many countries who fought against the Nazis. Of those, between 20,000 and 30,000 were Jewish. Most Jewish partisans were from Eastern Europe: Poland, Lithuania, and Latvia. The majority of

Jewish partisans fought alongside partisans from other countries, most often Russia, and also other religions. But some formed all-Jewish partisan groups.

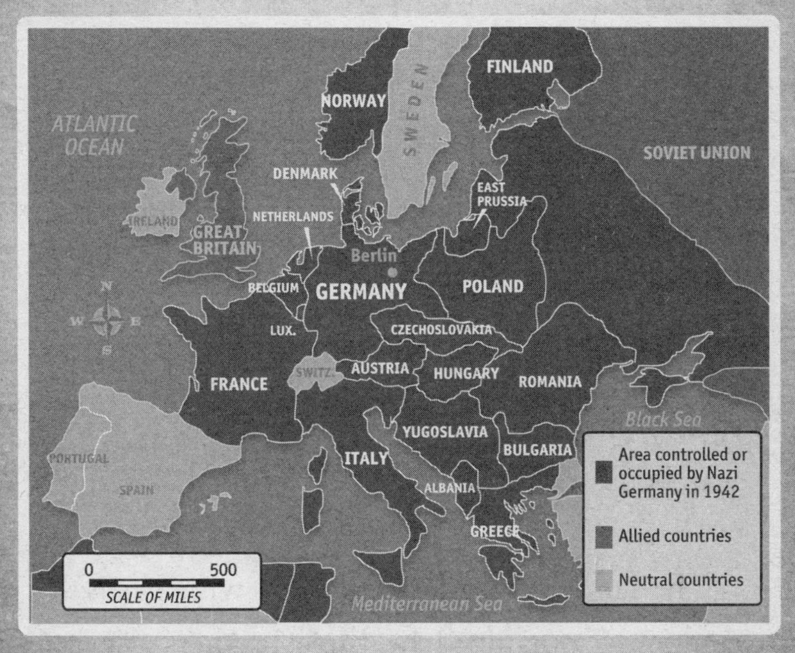

Courtesy of Scholastic Classroom Magazines

How did the partisans survive?

Just imagine trying to live in an enormous forest — without warm clothes, sleeping bags, or any special equipment. Then imagine that you're also being hunted by cold-blooded killers. This was what it meant to be a Jewish partisan. Most arrived in the forest with little more than the clothes on their backs, already weakened from hunger and the terrible suffering they'd experienced in ghettos. Few had any special training as fighters.

Those who survived were strong, resourceful, and lucky. They built secret camps deep in the forests, with underground dwellings that were almost invisible even to someone walking nearby. They scrounged for food, often forced to steal from local farmers or from Nazi food warehouses. Above all, they worked together to survive.

The largest and most famous Jewish partisan camp was organized by three brothers, Tuvia, Zus, and Asael Bielski. In addition to fighting Nazis, the Bielskis rescued more than 1,200 Jewish men, women, and children, and protected them at large partisan camps hidden deep in a forest.

How did a man as evil as Adolf Hitler become the leader of Germany?

This is a complicated subject; people have written entire books on it. But here's a simple enough answer: Germany in the 1930s was a sad and scary place. The country had lost World War I (a war they started, by the way). Many Germans felt humiliated by their defeat in that war. Life was very tough. A large number of Germans were poor and desperate. It was during this time that Adolf Hitler rose to power.

Hitler didn't seem like a monster at first. He seemed almost ridiculous, with his little mustache and strange way of waving his arm. People laughed at him.

But Hitler had a way about him — a power to almost hypnotize people. He was an incredible speaker. He stood in front of huge crowds of Germans and made big promises — that he would lead Germany back to strength. And many people, hungry for change, put their faith in him.

Why didn't Jewish people just leave Europe when Hitler came to power?

Some did manage to leave Germany and neighboring countries in the early years of Hitler's rule. But it wasn't easy. During the 1930s, as they do today, most nations had very strict rules about immigration. Some Jewish people moved, mostly to America, South America, and Palestine (which became the nation of Israel in 1948). But the majority of Jews had nowhere they could go. And after 1939, when World War II officially began, leaving Europe became even more difficult. By 1941, most Jewish people in Europe were imprisoned in ghettos or Nazi prison camps, and escape was almost impossible.

Were the Nazis punished for their crimes?

At the end of World War II, thousands of Nazis were captured and punished. Hitler and many Nazi leaders took their own lives when it became clear that Germany would lose the war. Hundreds of others were put on trial after the war. Most were found guilty and executed for their crimes.

But thousands of Nazis did manage to escape from Germany, including some responsible for planning the Holocaust. Most fled to South America and the United States. Over the decades, many of these criminals have been captured and brought to justice.

A TIME LINE OF THE HOLOCAUST AND WORLD WAR II

These are just a small number of important events that happened during this frightening and complex time in history.

1933

January 30: Hitler becomes chancellor of Germany.

September 22: Jews in Germany are banned from many jobs, including teaching in public schools, working on newspapers and in radio, and writing books.

1935

September 15: Nazis begin passing rules, known as the "Nuremburg Race Laws," that take away freedoms and rights from German Jews. For example, Jews in Germany are no longer permitted to attend public schools and colleges, marry people who are not Jewish, or join the military.

1938

November 9–10: Mobs of people attack Jewish-owned stores, businesses, and homes in Germany, Austria, and other Nazi-controlled areas. By morning, the streets are filled with glass from broken windows. The event becomes known as *Kristallnacht*, German for "The Night of Broken Glass." Violent mobs destroy 267 synagogues and roughly 7,500 shops and businesses in Germany.

1939

Nazis begin putting Jewish people in ghettos. By 1945, there will be more than 1,100 Jewish ghettos in Poland, Latvia, Lithuania and other Nazi-controlled areas.

September 1: Germany invades Poland.

September 3: World War II officially begins when Great Britain and France declare war on Germany.

1940

April 9–May 10: Germany invades Denmark, Norway, Holland, Belgium, France, and Luxembourg. Every Jewish person living in these areas is now in peril.

September 27: Japan joins forces with Germany and Italy. Together they become known as the "Axis Powers."

November 15: The Nazis create the largest Jewish ghetto, in Warsaw, Poland. Four hundred thousand Jewish people — almost one-third of the city's population — are crammed into tiny area. On average, 7 people live in every room.

1941

June 22: Germany invades Russia and its territories.

December 7: In a surprise attack, Japanese fighter pilots bomb US military bases at Pearl Harbor, Hawaii. The next day, the US declares war on Japan.

December 11: The United States declares war on Germany and Italy. It joins with Great Britain, Russia, and other countries to form the "Allied Powers."

1943

April 19: Jewish fighters in the Warsaw ghetto attack Nazis and police. Fighting lasts for about a month, until Germans destroy the entire ghetto.

October 1: Citizens in Denmark rescue more than 7,800 Danish Jews, ferrying them in fishing boats to Sweden, where they are safe.

1944

June 6: 160,000 Allied troops invade a Nazi-held area in Normandy, France. The day, known as D-day, marks a turning point in World War II as Allied troops begin to chase the Nazis back to Germany.

1945

Allied troops free hundreds of thousands of survivors from concentration camps.

April 30: Hitler takes his own life.

May 7: Germany surrenders.

August 6 and 9: U.S. drops atomic bombs on the Japanese cities of Hiroshima and Nagasaki.

September 2: Japan surrenders.
World War II officially ends.

1948

May 14: The nation of Israel is founded.

FOR MORE INFORMATION

For further information about Jewish partisans, including dozens of video interviews, go to the website of the Jewish Partisans Educational Foundation: www.JewishPartisans.org.

For more information about the Holocaust, explore the website of the United States Holocaust Museum: www.ushmm.org.

For recommendations for books to read about the Holocaust and Jewish partisans, go to my website: www.LaurenTarshis.com.

I SURVIVED

READ THEM ALL, THEN TAKE THE QUIZ TO TEST YOUR SURVIVAL SKILLS AT WWW.SCHOLASTIC.COM/ISURVIVED.